This Little Tiger book belongs to:

_____

_____

_____

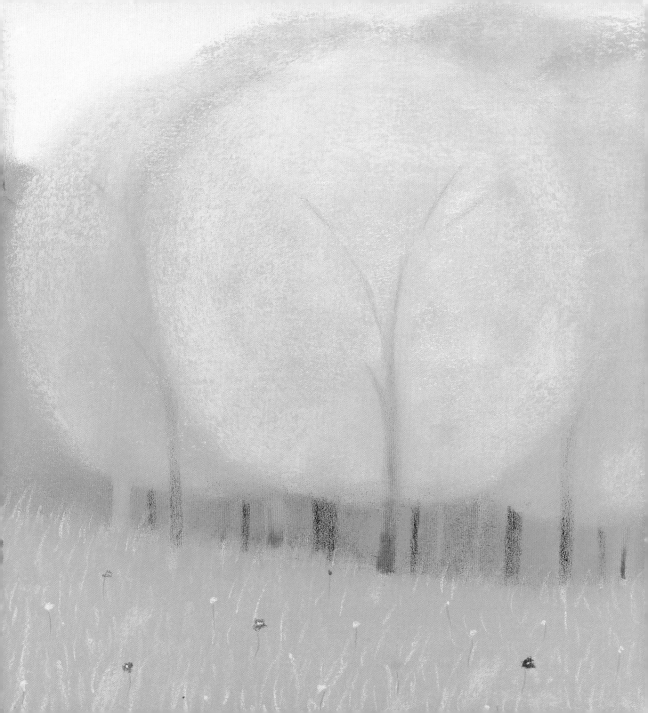

For Joey
— A. R.

To every child in this world who, because of war,
is deprived of a peaceful and playful childhood
— D. K.

LITTLE TIGER PRESS
An imprint of Magi Publications
1 The Coda Centre,
189 Munster Road, London SW6 6AW
www.littletigerpress.com

First published in Great Britain 2005
by Little Tiger Press, London
This edition published 2010

ISBN 978-1-84895-174-7

Printed in China

10 9 8 7 6 5 4 3 2 1

What Bear Likes Best!

by
Alison Ritchie

illustrated by
Dubravka Kolanovic

LITTLE TIGER PRESS

Bear was sunning himself on his
favorite hilltop.
He loved days like this –
nothing in particular to do and
nowhere in particular to go.

Buzzzzzzzzz!

Buzzzz! A bee
landed on his nose.

"Get up, Bear," he said crossly.

"How can I collect pollen with bears squashing my flowers?"

"Sorry, Bee," said Bear, laughing.

Bear curled himself up
and roly-polied down the hill.
Roly-polying was one of his
favorite things to do.

Yippeeeeeeeeeee!

Bump! Bear landed on top
of something warm and furry.
"Oi!" gasped Mole. "How can I
dig holes with bears landing on me?"

Oooof!

"I'll help you!" said Bear. And he dug
and dug and dug.

"Stop! Stop! STOP!" cried Mole,
as mud flew everywhere.

"Sorry, Mole," said Bear and he
hurried away.

Bear ran towards the river
and splashed into the water.
Splashing was one of his
favorite things to do.

Splish

Splash

"Hey!" grumbled Heron. "How can I catch
fish with bears chasing them away?"
"Sorry, Heron," said Bear and he
bounced off to play somewhere else.

Blah!

Bear hopped across the stepping stones,
leapt on to the riverbank and ran into
the woods. It was time for a back scratch.
Scratching his back was one of his
favorite things to do.

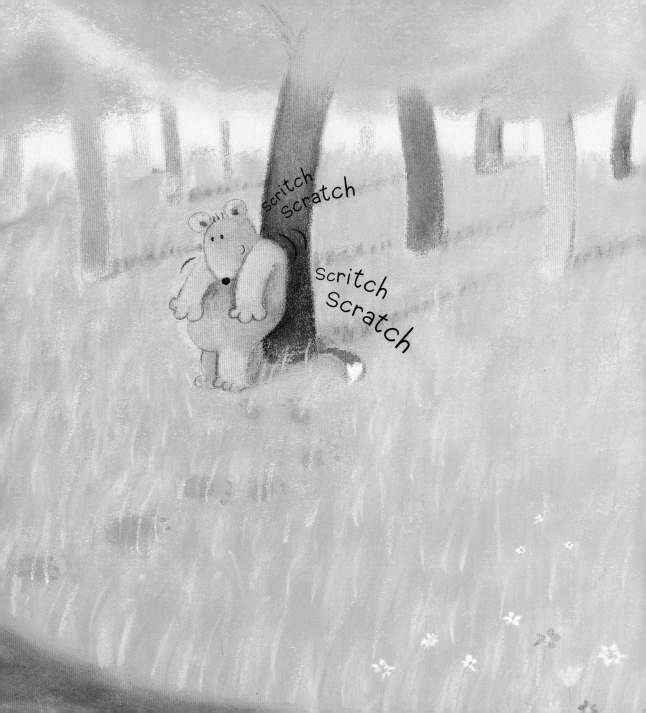

"Who's that?" said Fox, sleepily.
"How can I rest with bears
    shaking the trees?"

"Sorry, Fox," said Bear.
"Do you want to scratch
too? It's so nice!"
But Fox did not
want to scratch,
so Bear clambered
up the tree.

Wheeee!

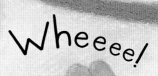

Wheeee!

Bear swung from branch to branch.
Swinging was one of his favorite
things to do.

Ooops!

Crash! Bear flew into a tree-trunk.

"Yikes!" cried Woodpecker, flying high into the air. "How can I peck holes with bears crashing into my tree!"

"Oops! Sorry!" cried Bear, jumping to the ground.

"Bother! Everyone's too busy to
play," Bear thought. "Oh, well!"
He skipped through the woods,
along the riverbank, across the field
and back to his favorite hilltop.

Bear lay sunning himself on the hilltop.

Suddenly he heard a loud BUZZZZZZZ!
"Oh no! I'm in trouble again," he thought.

He saw all his friends coming towards him.

"Bear," said Bee, "you're very big…"

"And heavy," said Mole.

"And noisy," said Heron.

"And pesky," said Fox.

"And clumsy," said Woodpecker…

"...But you're really fun.
Let's play!"

"Hoorah!" cried Bear.
Because playing with his friends
really was his favorite thing to do.

More fantastic reads from Little Tiger Press!

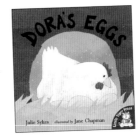

For information regarding any of the above titles or for our catalog, please contact us:
Little Tiger Press, 1 The Coda Centre, 189 Munster Road, London SW6 6AW, UK
Tel: +44 (0)20 7385 6333 • Fax: +44 (0)20 7385 7333 E-mail: info@littletiger.co.uk • www.littletigerpress.com